Change Order

Tana Reiff

A Pacemaker® *WorkTales* Book

FEARON/JANUS
Belmont, California

Simon & Schuster Supplementary Education Group

ℰ𝒲orkTales

A Robot Instead
The Easy Way
Change Order
Fighting Words
The Rip-Offs
The Right Type
The Saw that Talked
Handle with Care
The Road to Somewhere
Help When Needed

Cover illustration: Terry Hoff
Interior illustration: James Balkovek

ISBN 0-8224-7153-1
Library of Congress Catalog Card Number: 91-70781
Printed in the United States of America
1. 9 8 7 6 5 4 3 2

CONTENTS

Chapter 1 1

Chapter 2 7

Chapter 3 12

Chapter 4 19

Chapter 5 24

Chapter 6 31

Chapter 7 36

Chapter 8 43

Chapter 9 48

Chapter 10 55

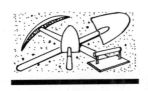

CHAPTER 1

"Hey, Adam!"
called Mel Harper.
"It's 5:00!
Time to call it a day!"

"I'll be right there,"
Adam Pratt called back.
"I want to take
another look
at these sidewalk plans."

"What's wrong with you?"
asked Mel.
"It's Friday, man!
Let's get
out of here!
Why are you
always finding
something else to do?"

"I'll tell you
all about it
at the bar,"
said Adam.
"Just wait five minutes.
That's all, OK?"

Adam and Mel worked
as concrete laborers
for a building company.
But they were
old buddies.
They had even gone
to school together.

Adam looked over
the sidewalk plans.
The new housing development
they were working on
was big.
The prints
showed a lot of sidewalk.
There was more
than Adam first knew about.
When he was finished,

he and Mel
headed for the bar.
Then Adam
began telling Mel
what was up.

"It's like this,"
he said.
"The company wants me
to be foreman
on a little concrete job
over at that new store.
You know me, Mel.
I really want
to be a foreman.
I always have.
The company
is giving me a break here.
So I need to get ready
for my first try at it.
I don't want
to mess up.
That's why
I'm taking a hard look
at everything we do.

It takes
a little extra time."

"I never did understand
why you want
to be a foreman, buddy,"
said Mel.
"I wouldn't
touch that job
with a ten-foot pole.
Being the one
between the workers
and the job super?
You can have it.
You like the idea
of more money, right?"

"The money
would be nice,"
said Adam.
"But the main thing is,
I'd rather be a foreman
than a laborer.
I want to *run* work,
not just do it."

"Hey, buddy,"
laughed Mel.
"Maybe someday
you'll be my foreman!
Wouldn't that be
big fun?"

"Sure would,"
Adam laughed back.
But he wasn't so sure
being Mel Harper's foreman
would be a good idea.
After all,
they were buddies.

Thinking It Over

1. Would you rather
   be a laborer
   or a foreman?

2. Have you ever worked
   with a good friend?
   What was it like?

3. What do you think
   would happen
   if Adam became
   Mel's foreman?

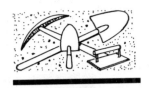

CHAPTER 2

Adam was foreman
on the small job
at the new store
for two weeks.
Mel missed him.
He liked working
with his buddy.
It was a lot of laughs.

More than that,
Mel needed Adam.
He didn't work as well
without Adam.
Mel was a good worker.
But he counted on Adam
to keep him moving.
He didn't mind
when Adam helped him
set forms just right.
Adam was always ready
with his tape measure.

He would measure
and measure again.
And Adam's finish work
was always beautiful.

Mel wasn't as careful
about his work.
But he did fine
as long as Adam
was around.
Adam made sure
that both of them
always looked good.

So the time
that Adam was away
was hard for Mel.
The foreman
found something wrong
with Mel's work
ten times a day.
Mel was glad
when Adam got back
from the other work site.
Now things

could get back
to the way they were.

But that is not
what happened.
Adam did come back.
Then, a week later,
the foreman left
for a new job.

The job super,
Dave True,
called Adam
into his office trailer.
"You did a great job
over at the store,"
Dave told Adam.
"As you know,
we now need
a new, full-time foreman.
The company
will go along
with the person I pick.
I've already put in
a good word for you.

So the job is yours
if you want it."

They were the words
Adam had waited to hear
for a long time.
"I want it,"
he said.

"Then let's go out there
and tell your crew,"
said Dave.

Thinking It Over

1. Do you need someone
   to help "keep you moving"?

2. Why can it be a good idea
   to test someone
   with a small job first?

3. What makes someone
   right for a foreman's job?

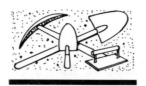

CHAPTER 3

When Adam
became foreman,
things changed.
Before, Adam
would have helped Mel
get the job done right.
Now, Adam just
gave orders.
"Do this!
Do that!
Get it right!"
he often shouted.

Before, Adam
would have shown Mel
the best way
to dig out sidewalk
and stone it in.
Now he just told him
to get it done.

Like before,
Adam was out there
with his tape measure
all the time.
But now,
if something was off,
Adam would say
it was wrong,
instead of helping
to get it right.

When it was time
to pour the concrete,
Adam didn't help Mel
to place it nice and flat.
Now he shouted at Mel
if the concrete
wasn't placed right.

Mel didn't like
Adam's new ways.
His buddy Adam
had become the boss.
He didn't like
taking orders

from Adam.
And Adam
seemed to enjoy
giving a lot of orders.
Having Adam
as the foreman
just did not feel right
to Mel.
He felt
like a little kid
in school.
Rather than try
to do his work right,
Mel only felt like
giving the teacher trouble.

"Hey, Adam!"
Mel called.
"Come over here a minute!
We have a question."

Adam walked over
to Mel and the other guys.
"What's the problem?"
he said.

"See this drain?"
Mel asked.
"I think
it's sitting too high.
When we pour the concrete,
it's going to stick up."

"You'll have to lower it,"
said Adam.
"You'll have to dig it out.
Then lower it
about half an inch."

With that,
Adam walked away.
He was
a working foreman.
He had work to do
on another sidewalk.

Mel looked
at the other guys.
"Does he know
what he's asking us
to do?

I don't see
how we can dig out
that drain.
I say,
let's not do it
and say we did.
Adam's my buddy.
He won't care
if it's off
by only half an inch."

"Fine with me,"
said Harry Groff.
"I sure don't want
to dig out
a lot of stone and dirt
just to lower a drain
by half an inch!"

"Well, then, good buddies,
I guess we're finished!"
laughed Mel.

The next day,
they poured the concrete.

They placed it
across the stone
the best they could.
But the drain
stuck out
half an inch.
Everyone could see it.

    Mel was wrong.
Adam did care.

Thinking It Over

1. What makes
   a good leader?

2. Would you have trouble
   taking orders from a friend?

3. How hard
   would you work
   to get a job done right?
   What is it worth to you
   to get something right?

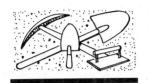

CHAPTER 4

The drain problem
was Adam's first test
as a foreman.
He felt as if
he had failed.
He told himself
he should have checked
the drain
before the concrete
was poured.
He couldn't believe
his buddy Mel
would try getting over on him
like this.
He would have to tell Mel
and the others
what was what.

"Now, you all listen up,"
Adam began.

"I used to be
one of you.
I still am.
We're all
making the sidewalk
for these new homes.
But now
I'm the foreman.
That means
when I tell you
to do something,
it's your job
to get it done.
Does everyone understand?"

"Sure, sure,"
said Harry Groff.

"I'll listen to you,
all right,"
Mel laughed.
"Over a beer tonight,
that's when!"

All four guys
on the crew
laughed with Mel.
Adam wasn't laughing.

"I don't think
you got my meaning,"
said Adam.
"We're here
to do a job right.
And we are all
going to do it."

"Listen to Mr. Boss Man!"
laughed Mel.
"He's got
some strong talk for us,
doesn't he now?"

"Cut it out, Mel!"
Adam shouted.
"We may be buddies
from way back.

But I'm talking
about work here.
Got it?"

The crew
said nothing.

"Now let's get working!"
Adam said.
"I'll be checking
your finish work
in one hour."

Thinking It Over

1. Have you ever ganged up
    against someone?
    Why did you do it?

2. Do you ever give anyone
    "back talk"?
    Why or why not?

3. How do you feel
    when you know
    someone will be checking
    your work?

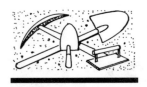

CHAPTER 5

The crew
got back to work.
Five minutes later,
Mel called Adam over.

"Hey, buddy!"
said Mel.
"How am I doing here?
Am I doing this right?
I just couldn't wait
one whole hour
to find out!"

"You're doing fine,"
said Adam.
"And you can stop
giving me trouble
right now.
I don't need it."

Five minutes later,
Mel called Adam over again.

"How am I doing now?"
he asked.

"It could be a little smoother
down at that end,"
said Adam.

"Is that so?"
said Mel.
"Well, I'll just have
to fix that right up,
won't I?
After all,
you're the foreman!"

Harry and the others
heard Mel talking.
"You tell him!"
they shouted.
"A foreman's a foreman,
and we got a good one!"

Everyone laughed.
Adam walked away.

Another five minutes
went by.
Mel called Adam over
yet again.
"What is it this time?"
Adam asked him.

"I just can't tell
if I'm doing this right,"
said Mel.
"Why don't you tell me
what I'm doing wrong."

"That sidewalk
looks good and flat now,"
said Adam.
"Just keep on doing
what you're doing."

"Tell me
what I'm doing,"
Mel begged.

"You're ragging me, Mel,"
said Adam.
"Give it a rest."

"I'm not ragging you,"
Mel answered back.
"I want you to
tell me
what I'm doing."

"Stop pushing me,"
said Adam.

Then Mel
got up into Adam's face.
"Tell me
what I'm doing,
Adam Pratt.
You're the foreman."

Adam had had enough.
He was angry
past reason.
He backed off
a few inches.

Then he landed a blow
squarely on Mel's face.

The hit
surprised Mel.
He stood there
for a second.
Then he dropped
his steel trowel
and hit Adam back.
Before they knew it,
Adam and Mel were
on the ground,
fighting like dogs.

"Hey, you guys!"
called Harry Groff.
"Cool out!
Cool out!"
He pulled Mel
away from Adam.
Everyone was surprised
to see Adam get this mad.

Just then,
Dave True
showed up.
"What's going on here?"
he shouted.
"Harry, take care of Mel.
Adam, come with me."

Adam stood up.
He brushed off
the stones and dirt
from his clothes.
He walked
into the trailer
with the super.
Now he felt like
a dog
with its tail
between its legs.
He was sure
he was about
to get fired.

Thinking It Over

1. Has anyone
   ever pushed you too far?
   What does it take
   to push you too far?

2. Does a fight
   help matters or hurt matters?

3. What are you thinking
   when you see
   other people fighting?

4. Do you ever
   lose your cool?
   If so,
   are you sorry later or not?

CHAPTER 6

"No, I'm not going to
fire you,"
Dave told Adam.
"Why don't you tell me
what's going on?"

"I'm trying
to get this job done right,"
said Adam.
"But the crew
won't listen to me.
All they want to do
is give me a hard time.
I tried
some strong talk
with them.
But it only flew
right back in my face.
They're having fun

making my job very hard.
And I really don't know
what to do about it."

"Would it help
if I moved Mel Harper
to another crew?"
asked Dave.

"He's my buddy, Dave,"
said Adam.
"I always liked
working with him."

"You don't like it much
these days,
do you?"
Dave asked.

"No," said Adam.
"Guess I don't.
But Mel doesn't want
to leave Harry
and the guys.
I have another idea.

Why don't you put me
back down on the crew?
Find a new foreman.
Maybe everyone
would be happier
if I were a laborer again.
You know,
just like the old days."

   "You don't mean that,"
said Dave.
"You always wanted
to be a foreman.
Now you are one.
You just have to learn
how to handle the job.
But Mel Harper
is making life
hard for you.
I'll tell you what.
I'm going to let you
get started
on a brand-new job.
It's a group
of new office buildings.

You'll have
a whole different crew.
We'll see
how Mel and the guys act
under a different foreman.
If they give him trouble,
they'll be
in trouble with me.
Without Mel around,
you'll probably
become a better foreman.
And you and Mel
can go back
to being buddies.
What do you say?"

   "Let's try it,"
answered Adam.
"If it doesn't work,
then you can fire me!"

   "Get out of here!"
said Dave.
"I'm not letting you
off that easy."

Thinking It Over

1. Why do you think
   Dave did not fire Adam?

2. Do you think Adam
   should have gone back
   on the crew
   and stayed on as foreman?

3. How could Adam
   better handle
   the job of foreman?

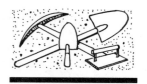

CHAPTER 7

Three Fridays went by
before Mel and Adam
saw each other again.
Adam's work site
was miles away
from the housing development.

It was Adam's idea
to meet at the bar.
Fridays hadn't been the same
without that good time.
He called Mel
to break the ice
between them.
They made plans
to meet after work.

Adam got there first.
He sat at the bar.
He ordered a beer.

Just then,
he felt a tap
on his back.
He turned around.
He expected to see Mel.
But it was Harry.

"Hey, Adam,
how's it going?"
Harry asked him.
"We don't see you
these days.
Where are you working?"

Adam told Harry
about the new office buildings.
Work was just starting.
Digging sidewalk
had not even begun.

Then Mel walked in.
Adam didn't want Harry
hanging around.
He wanted
to talk to Mel alone.

Harry didn't walk away.
He and Mel
started talking
about the housing development.
They seemed pretty happy
with the way
the work was going.
They talked on and on.
Adam just sat there.

Three beers later,
Adam stood up.
"Well, guys,"
he said,
"I'd better head home.
Nice seeing you."

"Hey, man,"
said Mel.
"Wait a minute.
I want to talk with you.
Harry, later, man."

"You and Harry
seem to be good buddies

these days,"
said Adam.

"You know how it is,"
said Mel.
"We work together.
It's kind of like
you and me
used to be.
He helps me out.
I get the job done."

"That sounds great,"
said Adam.
"Do you think
you and I
will ever work together again?"

"Look, man,
I'm sorry
about giving you
such a hard time,"
said Mel.
"There we were,
all those years,

working together like buddies.
All of a sudden,
you're the boss.
I couldn't handle that."

"It wasn't all you,"
said Adam.
"Maybe I came on
a little too strong."

"Maybe you did,"
said Mel.
"You were throwing out orders
like there was no tomorrow.
Maybe we were both
a little uptight.
Hey, man,
I miss you, buddy."

"You know,
I sure could use
you and Harry
over at the office buildings.
When will you be done
at the housing development?"

"In a few weeks,"
said Mel.
"Do you think
you could get both of us
put on your crew?"

On Monday morning,
Adam went
to talk over the idea
with Dave True.

Thinking It Over

1. If you had a fight
   with someone,
   who would make
   the first move
   to patch things up?

2. What do you do
   when you're feeling left out?

3. Why do you think
   Mel and Harry have become
   buddies?

4. Why does it help
   to talk over problems?

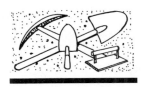

CHAPTER **8**

Mel and Harry
came over
to work at the offices.
They joined
Adam's crew.
Dave True
also came over
to be the job super.
They all
had a big job
ahead of them.

The first step
was to dig out for sidewalk.
Adam put Mel
on the backhoe.
He knew
Mel liked that job.

And he knew
Mel was good at it.

When the sidewalk
was all dug out,
it was time
to set the forms
along the sides.
Mel needed a little help
with that job.
Adam showed him
how to set forms right.
Then he let Harry
help Mel
to keep on going.
Adam kept an eye
on their work.
He didn't shout orders
all day long.
He only made sure
everyone knew
what to do.

Next, it was time
to stone in the sidewalk.

Mel had no trouble
with that job, either.
He and Harry and Adam
all worked together.

Everything about the job
was going fine.
The crew was working
fast and right.
Then one morning,
Dave True came over
to talk with Adam.
"Bad news,"
said Dave.
"I just got
a change order
on this job.
They want the sidewalk
six inches wider
than we're doing it."

"You must be kidding!"
cried Adam.
"We've got the forms
almost all set!"

"I know,"
said Dave.
"But the change order
says six inches wider.
You're just going
to have to move the forms out
six inches."

Adam went back
to tell the crew.
He didn't want
to move the forms
any more than they did.
It would mean
bringing in the backhoe again.
It would put the job behind
by weeks.
But Adam's job
was to make those walks
six inches wider.

Thinking It Over

1. In what ways
   is Adam becoming a better
   foreman?

2. How do you feel
   when you are asked
   to do something
   all over again?

3. Why is there such a thing
   as a change order?

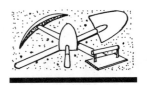

CHAPTER 9

"Move the forms?"
cried Mel
when Adam explained
the change order.
"What difference
does it make
if the walks
aren't six inches wider?
Are they trying
to kill us, or what?"

"We don't
own this place,"
said Adam.
"We're only building it.
So let's get moving!"

"What if we don't?"
Mel asked.

"Move the forms,"
ordered Adam.
"Just start at the beginning
and keep on moving.
I don't need
crying babies.
I need strong men
to move those forms out."

"I say,
let's keep the sidewalk
the way it is,"
said Mel.
"Any new walk
we put in
can be six inches wider."

"Forget it,"
said Adam.

"I hate change orders,"
said Mel.
"Just like I hate
the change in order

in who's foreman.
Know what I mean?"
He began to laugh.

Adam didn't laugh.
He marched right over
to Dave's trailer.
"I've had it!"
he shouted.
"I can't take
the back talk.
I quit!"
With that,
he marched
off the work site.

Adam didn't show up
the next morning.
Even so,
Mel and Harry and the crew
worked on moving the forms.

No one heard a word
from Adam.

No one could reach him
by phone.
Then, three days later,
he answered the phone
when Mel called.

"I was wrong,"
Mel told Adam.
"You are the foreman.
You told us
to move the forms.
It's my job
to do what you say."

"I was wrong, too,"
said Adam.
"I can't let
a hot head like you
get to me.
If I'm ever going to make it
as a foreman,
I can't let you
get the better of me.
I'm going to see

if I can get
my job back."

He went
to see Dave True.
"I want
one more try,"
said Adam.
"Being a foreman
is much harder
than I counted on.
But I'm seeing
my weak spots.
I know
I can do better."

"I told you
I wouldn't let you quit,"
said Dave.
"I'd be glad
to give you
one more try.
You show me
you can be a foreman.

I'll help you
in any way I can.
But if you walk off again,
I'll let you go."

Adam went out
to the crew.
There they were,
moving the forms.
It was a long, hard job.
But it was getting done.

Thinking It Over

1. Suppose you are Mel.
   Why did you start
   giving Adam a hard time
   again?

2. Do you think
   Adam should have quit?
   Why or why not?

3. Do you think
   Dave should have given Adam
   another try as foreman?
   Why or why not?

CHAPTER **10**

Adam and his crew
worked at that site
for the next year.
They caught up
after the change order.
They were even
a few weeks
ahead of the game.
The first businesses moved in
before all the offices
were finished.

On the last day there,
Mel was finishing
the last walk.
He looked up.
"Hey, Adam!"
he called.
"Come over here."

Adam came over.
There had been no trouble
since the day he walked off.
He hoped that Mel
wasn't starting trouble now.

"I want to do something
I've never done before!"
said Mel.
"I want
to sign my work.
How about you?"
He handed Adam
a sharp stone.

"If Dave True caught us,
he'd have our heads,"
laughed Adam.
He took the stone.
In the wet concrete,
back in the corner,
he wrote "A. P."
for Adam Pratt.
Mel wrote "M. H."
for Mel Harper.

"I must say,
that felt good,"
said Adam.
"We did
a real fine job here,
you and me."

"You talk as if
we built
this whole place
on our own!"
laughed Mel.

"I know we didn't,"
said Adam.
"I only mean
this was our first job
after the big change."

"The big change?"
asked Mel.
"With Adam Pratt
as a foreman
and Mel Harper
on his crew?"

"Yes," said Adam.
"We did it.
And we'll do it again."

They looked around
the whole group
of office buildings.
People were walking
on the sidewalks
Mel and Adam had built.
These people might never
look down and wonder
who built those walks.
But Adam Pratt and Mel Harper
knew the whole story.